Crinkleroot's GUIDE TO KNOWING THE TREES

BY JIM ARNOSKY

BRADBURY PRESS   *New York*

Maxwell Macmillan Canada   *Toronto*
Maxwell Macmillan International
New York   Oxford   Singapore   Sydney

Bradbury Press
Macmillan Publishing Company
866 Third Avenue
New York, NY 10022

Maxwell Macmillan Canada, Inc.
1200 Eglinton Avenue East, Suite 200
Don Mills, Ontario M3C 3N1

Macmillan Publishing Company is part of the
Maxwell Communication Group of Companies.
Printed and bound in the United States of America
10 9 8 7 6 5 4 3 2
The text of this book is set in ITC Bookman Medium.
The illustrations are rendered in pen-and-ink and watercolor.

In order to provide picture-book quality stock at an affordable price
and still save trees, this book is printed on paper composed of not less
than 50 percent recycled material, which includes pulp and other
by-products of the papermaking process that had, in the past, often
been discarded.

LIBRARY OF CONGRESS CATALOGING-IN-PUBLICATION DATA
Arnosky, Jim.
Crinkleroot's guide to knowing the trees / by Jim Arnosky. — 1st ed.
p.   cm.
Summary: An illustrated introduction to trees and woodlands with
information on how to identify the bark and the leaves, the many
ways that animals use trees, and how to read the individual history
that shapes every tree.
ISBN 0-02-705855-7
1. Trees—Juvenile literature.   2. Trees—Identification—Juvenile
literature.   3. Forest ecology—Juvenile literature.   [1. Trees.
2. Trees—Identification.   3. Forest ecology.   4. Ecology.]
I. Title.
QK475.8.A76   1992
582.16—dc20   91-18651

FOR HEATHER
TO READ TO
BILLY AND BEN

Greetings, friend! My name is Crinkleroot. You've found me in the middle of the forest. I've been walking through the woods, visiting with the trees. If you like, I'll introduce you. Some, like the giant oak trees, are among my oldest friends. Others, like these tiny new oak trees, are just starting out in life.

You couldn't have a better guide to the trees. I was born in a tree! I live in the forest, a place of many trees. There are trees growing where you live, too—in lawns and parks, by city sidewalks, in swampy places, meadows, and fields, even in the desert—anywhere there is soil, water, and sunlight.

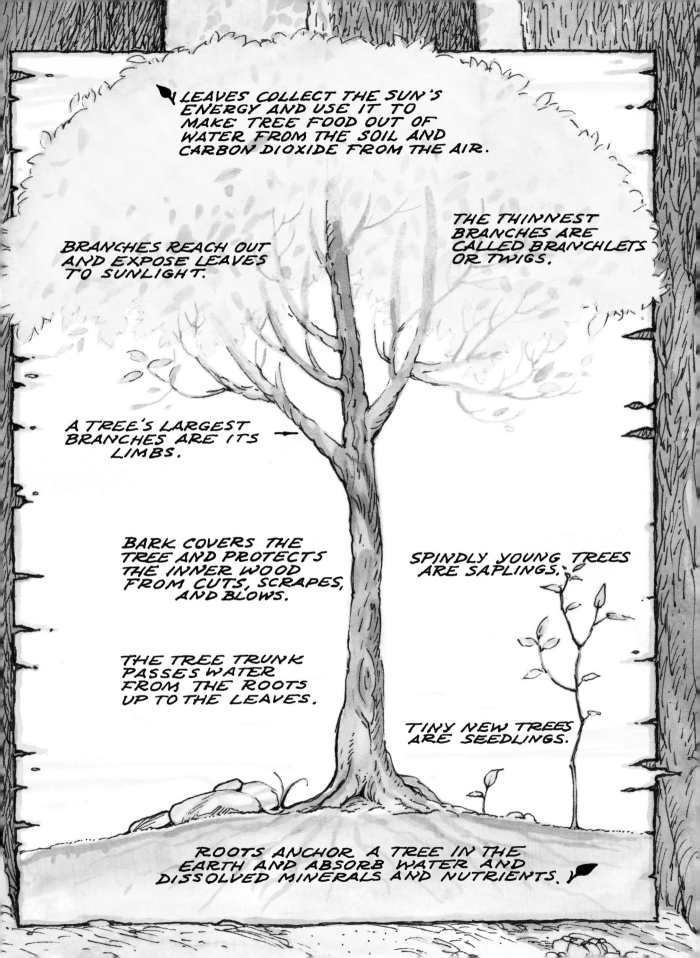

MAPLE SEEDLING

Maple, oak, birch, gum, ash, sassafras, and beech trees all have broad, flat leaves that are shed each autumn. Broad-leafed trees grow new leaves every spring.

SPRUCE SEEDLING

Cedar, pine, spruce, cypress, and fir trees are all evergreens. They keep their needle-shaped leaves all through the year and stay green even in winter.

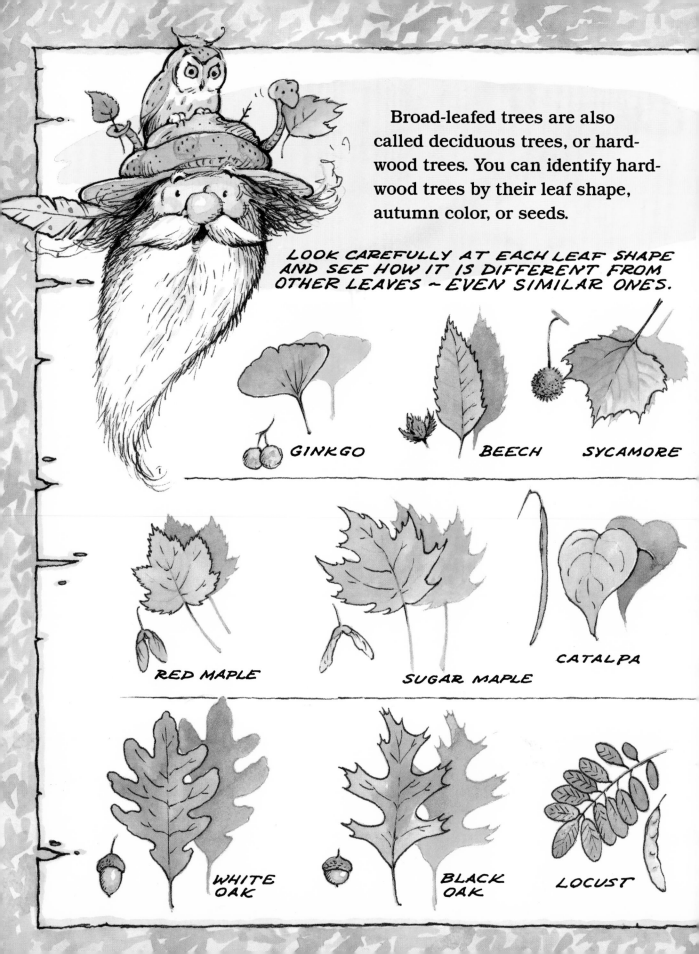

Broad-leafed trees are also called deciduous trees, or hardwood trees. You can identify hardwood trees by their leaf shape, autumn color, or seeds.

LOOK CAREFULLY AT EACH LEAF SHAPE AND SEE HOW IT IS DIFFERENT FROM OTHER LEAVES ~ EVEN SIMILAR ONES.

GINKGO

BEECH

SYCAMORE

RED MAPLE

SUGAR MAPLE

CATALPA

WHITE OAK

BLACK OAK

LOCUST

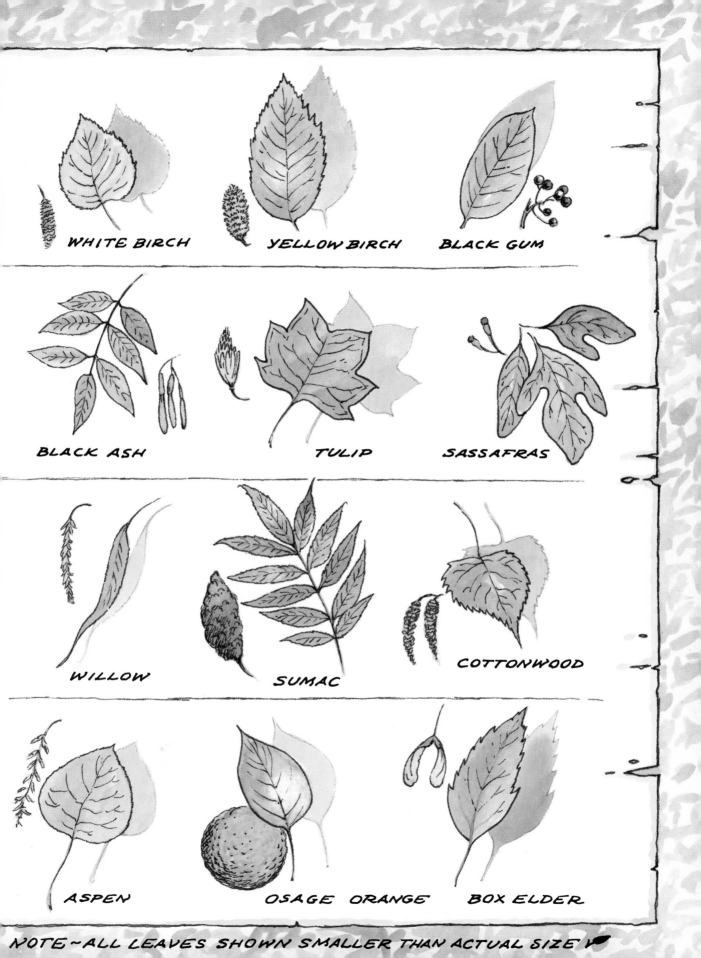

WHITE BIRCH

YELLOW BIRCH

BLACK GUM

BLACK ASH

TULIP

SASSAFRAS

WILLOW

SUMAC

COTTONWOOD

ASPEN

OSAGE ORANGE

BOX ELDER

NOTE ~ ALL LEAVES SHOWN SMALLER THAN ACTUAL SIZE

Evergreen trees are also called conifer trees, or softwood trees. You can identify softwood trees either by their needles or by their seed cones.

PINES HAVE LONG NEEDLES

PINE BOUGH

THAT GROW IN CLUSTERS OF 2 TO 5.

PINECONES

SPRUCE NEEDLES

SPRUCE CONES

SPRUCE BOUGH

FIR NEEDLES GROW IN A SEMICIRCLE ON THE NEEDLE TWIG.

FIR BOUGH

FIR CONES

HEMLOCK NEEDLES GROW ONE ON EITHER SIDE OF THE NEEDLE TWIG.

HEMLOCK BOUGH

HEMLOCK CONES ARE VERY SMALL.

CEDARS ALL HAVE SCALES INSTEAD OF NEEDLES.

CEDAR BOUGH AND CONE

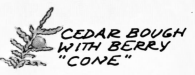

CEDAR BOUGH WITH BERRY "CONE"

TAMARACK NEEDLES ARE SHORT AND GROW IN BUNCHES.

THE TAMARACK CONIFER TREE CHANGES COLOR IS THE ONLY THAT IN FALL.

TAMARACK CONE

A forest of softwood trees is a mysterious-looking place. Long rays of sunlight shine down between tall, pointed treetops. Sounds are muffled by the evergreen boughs. The air is fragrant and still.

A hardwood forest is an open, airy place.
Breezes carry the scent of green leaves and bark.
Spots of sunlight dapple the tree trunks. Noises
echo sharply as they bounce off the hardwood
trees. Brittle fallen leaves crackle under
your step.

The ideal woods for wildlife has a rich variety of trees of all ages, shapes, and sizes. In a mixed woods there are a number of levels—"floors" where different animals can find living space.

Look in the highest treetops...

in the middle limbs and branches...

and near or on the ground.

In a mixed woods, seedlings, saplings, and mature
broad-leafed trees and evergreens produce a variety
of food that wildlife can eat the year round.

IN SPRING ANIMALS EAT
TENDER NEW SHOOTS OF
SEEDLINGS AND SAPLINGS.

ALL SUMMER LONG
THERE ARE JUICY
GREEN LEAVES.

FALL IS THE SEASON FOR TREE SEEDS AND NUTS.

IN WINTER ANIMALS EAT THE TINY WINTER-BUDS THAT HAVE FORMED ON THE LEAFLESS BRANCHES.

Besides food, trees provide wildlife with all-important cover for hiding—in the shadows trees cast, amid tree leaves and branches, behind tree trunks, inside hollow stumps, and in the dark earthen tunnels under exposed tree roots.

Dying or dead but still standing trees are as important to wildlife as healthy living trees. This hollow tree trunk is home to scores of wood-boring insects, which are food for raccoons, opossums, skunks, bears, and of course, woodpeckers! The many deep holes in the rotted wood excavated by animals searching for insects make dandy nesting holes for chickadees and tree-climbing mice. Squirrels use the high, dry holes to store seeds and pinecones.

Wherever a tree falls in the forest, a small, open, sunlit area is created. Sunny clearings in the woods are good places to look for grouse, turkeys, and other wildlife that like to eat and rest in warmth while remaining close to woodland cover.

And fallen old trees make way for new trees—the future forest—to sprout and grow.

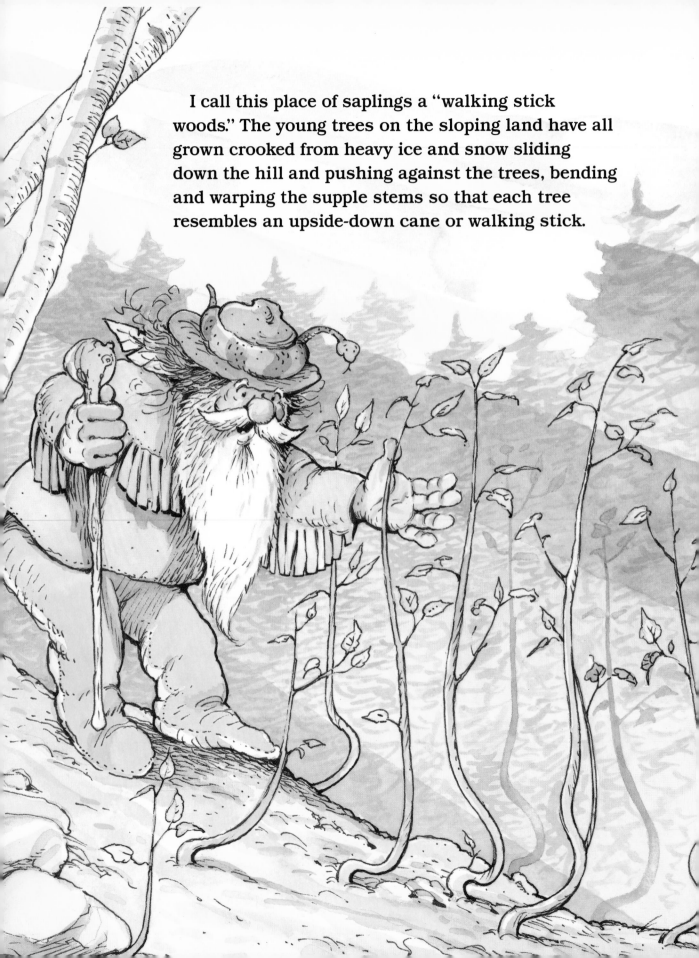

I call this place of saplings a "walking stick woods." The young trees on the sloping land have all grown crooked from heavy ice and snow sliding down the hill and pushing against the trees, bending and warping the supple stems so that each tree resembles an upside-down cane or walking stick.

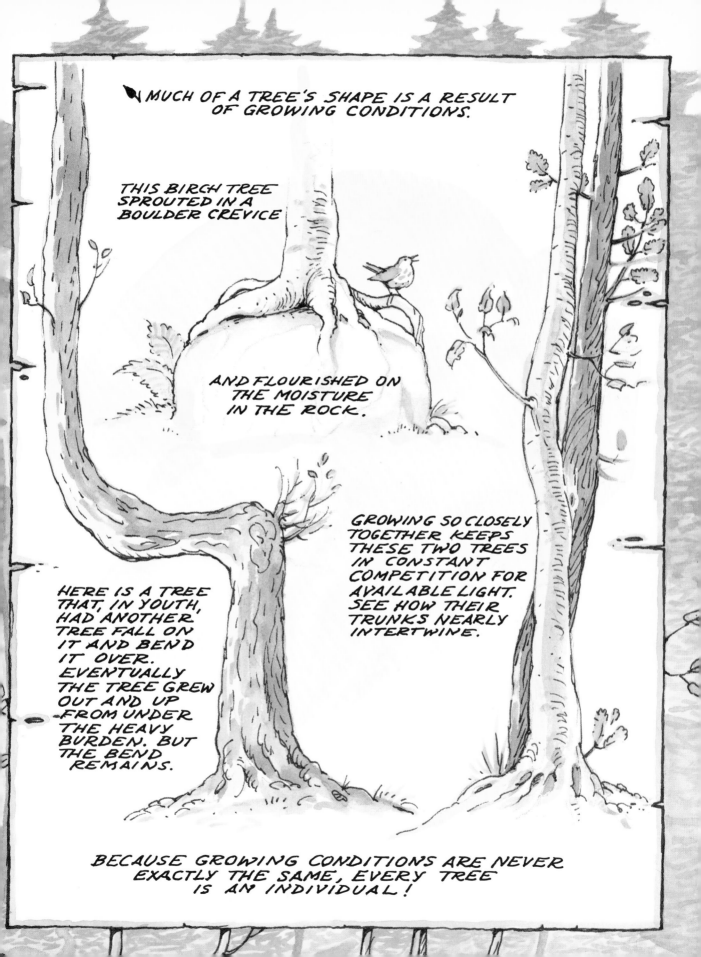

Best of all, I love the grand old
trees. Hemlocks or redwoods towering
straight and tall. And broad-trunked,
rough-barked maples and oaks, with
massive limbs reaching outward all
around.

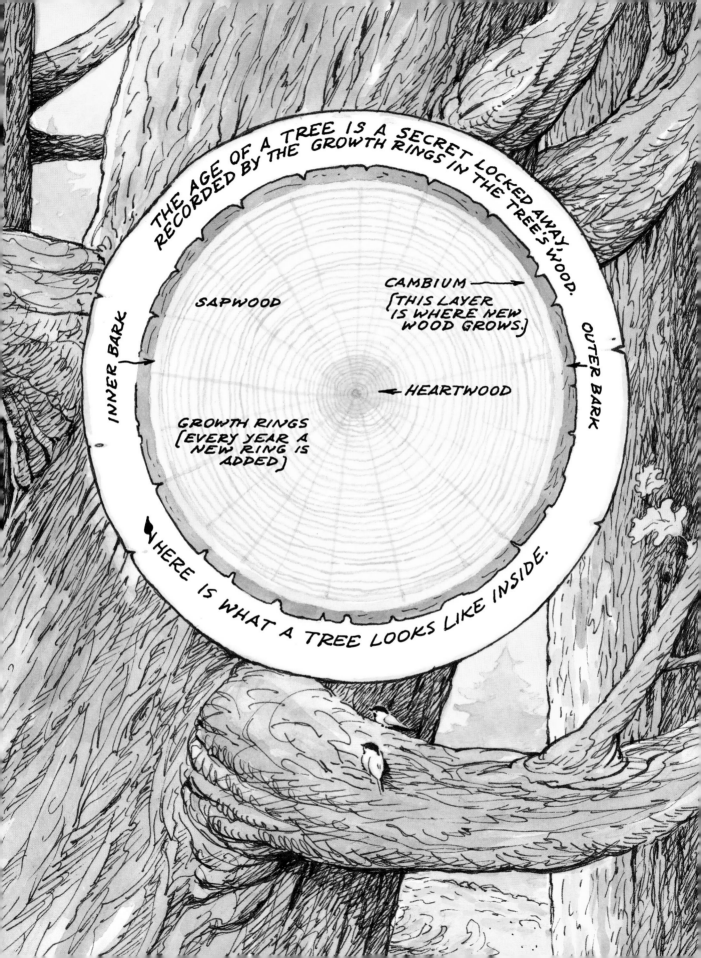

Wherever you live, there are trees standing patiently, waiting for you to come along and get to know them. On your next walk, spend a little time learning something about each individual tree you meet. Soon you'll know as many different trees as I do. Then, like me, whenever you walk into the woods, you'll be among old friends.

Crinkleroot was named after a wild-flower. He tells you where he lives—in the deepest part of the forest—in *I Was Born in a Tree and Raised by Bees*.

He can hear a fox turn in the forest and spot a molehill on a mountain. He can find an owl in daytime, and in *Crinkleroot's Book of Animal Tracking* he shows you how you can, too.

Most days, when Crinkleroot wakes up, his feet are itching to take him places —and you're invited to come along. In fact, *Horn Book Magazine* called *Crinkleroot's Guide to Walking in Wild Places* "a grand invitation to enjoy the natural world."

All of the Crinkleroot books are published by Bradbury Press.